Marley's Adventures in DREAMLAND

By Robin Killoran

Dedicated to Tiffany, Amara, and Marley. The three of you have impacted my life more than you will ever know.

Let me share a story of a boy,
who is sure to warm your heart within.
With his big smile so full of joy,
meet Mister Marley and let's begin.

Having fun is his number one,
like most other kids his age.
With all his games, he loves to run
and with toys he loves to play.

But there's something Marley truly dreads,
as it takes his fun away.
And that's to fall asleep or lie in bed.
Why must bedtime follow every day?

9

Well, clearly Marley does not know...

An incredible place is just so near!

It's called Dreamland, would you like to go?

Just fall asleep and it shall appear!

Forget about his toys for a while,
Marley could play with a real dinosaur!
A T-Rex with a great big smile,
they run through the jungle to go explore!

These toy cars are only so much fun,
imagine speeding around a track for real!
Marley's in first place and the race is done.
A champion, how does it feel?

And what good are superhero movies,
if Marley could be a hero of his own!
Super Marley, stopping bad guys with ease.
To the whole wide world he is known!

The excitement is building inside young Marley's head,
eager to see what adventures he will find.
He has one concern though and this he then said,
"What about the nightmares that I've seen in my mind?"

The nightmares that you speak of
come from The Scary Place, you see.
Not from the Dreamland that we love,
but from just across the street.

DREAM LAND

SCARY PLACE

It's true some monsters call it home
and they might trick you to come inside.
But don't be frightened or feel alone,
they aren't that tough - although they try.

DREAM LAND

If you ever do end up in The Scary Place,
just remember what I said on this day.
Look the silly monster right in his face,
put your hands to your head and then say...

"NANA NANA, BOO BOO. I AM NOT AFRAID OF YOU!"
Then stick out your tongue for good measure.
Scare him so much he just might turn blue,
then run back to Dreamland with pleasure!

The monster's long gone, a lesson was taught,
so there isn't a reason to stress.
Stay positive, think happy thoughts,
this night's already been a success.

Marley is so happy to hear this news,
closing his eyes as he jumps into bed.
Thinking happy thoughts while he's waiting to snooze,
excited for the adventure ahead.

And this goes for every girl and boy,
not just my dear friend Marley.
Drift off to Dreamland and enjoy
because tomorrow comes so sharply.

And when the morning comes back around,
it's true you may not remember,
but do not let this bring you down
for every night will be an adventure.

About the Author

Robin Killoran

First time author born and raised in British Columbia, Canada. On a mission to help parents everywhere get their kids to sleep at a reasonable hour! Started this project when a remarkable young man came into my life and inspired me with his disdain for bedtime. Fingers crossed that this book will have an impact on him and others alike!

Made in the USA
Columbia, SC
23 July 2021